Nature's Great Balancing Act

Nature's Great
Balancing Act
IN OUR OWN BACKYARD

E. Jaediker Norsgaard

PHOTOGRAPHS BY
Campbell Norsgaard

COBBLEHILL BOOKS
Dutton • New York

Library of Congress Cataloging-in-Publication Data
Norsgaard, E. Jaediker (Ernestine Jaediker)
Nature's great balancing act : in our own backyard / E. Jaediker Norsgaard ;
photographs by Campbell Norsgaard.
p.   cm.
"Cobblehill books" — T.p.
Summary: Discusses the interrelationship of all the creatures and plants in
nature, emphasizing the importance of insects.
ISBN 0-525-65028-8
1. Ecology—Juvenile literature.   [1. Ecology.   2. Insects.]   I. Title.
QH541.14.N67   1990
574.5—dc20   89-38589   CIP

Published in the United States by Cobblehill Books,
an affiliate of Dutton Children's Books, a division
of Penguin Books USA Inc.
Published simultaneously in Canada by
Fitzhenry & Whiteside Limited, Toronto
Designed by Jean Krulis
Printed in Hong Kong
First Edition   10 9 8 7 6 5 4 3 2 1

To Meryl Streep,
who out of profound concern for the environment, donated her talent to narrate the video version of *Nature's Great Balancing Act*. In her own words, "I feel the greatest gift we can give our children is an understanding of and reverence for the natural world."

Contents

Welcome to our backyard! You won't find a tame grass carpet, but a large semi-wild wonderland that stretches from our house to the bordering woods. Some years ago we decided to let everything grow as it pleases. Now it's a community where many of our fellow creatures are at home. On a summer day, grasshoppers will jump away from your footsteps. You'll see bees buzzing around raspberry bushes, butterflies landing on wildflowers, birds feeding insects to their young. There are chipmunks and a family of bold raccoons. Deer venture out of the woods to nibble hedges and shrubs.

All creatures in the animal kingdom depend on plants and on each other for survival, one feeding on another. Many plants depend on insects for help in reproduction. They are all parts of a gigantic puzzle in which the pieces fit together but, like a kaleidoscope, are forever changing. You are a mammal, and you are a part of that puzzle too, though you are quite different from other mammals and from birds, reptiles, amphibians, and insects. All living things are members of nature's great balancing act. You can see how this works right here in our own backyard.

GREEN PLANTS AND YOU

Look around at the leafy green plants bathed in sunlight. If green plants stopped producing oxygen and food, life as we know it would end.

Take a deep breath. You are inhaling oxygen that was released by green plants. In return, you exhale carbon dioxide which the plants take in. In this way, animals and plants are partners.

Green plants on land and in the water are the basis of all the food you and other animals eat—either directly or in a food chain. Animals get the energy to move, grow, reproduce, and the materials to create all the substances that make up their bodies by eating plants or other animals that have eaten plants.

That's because only green plants have the talent to capture the sun's energy and transform it into food. In a process called *photosynthesis*, green chlorophyll in leaves uses energy from the sun to split water molecules that the plant takes up from the ground. These water molecules are split into hydrogen and oxygen, and the oxygen is released into the air. The hydrogen combines with carbon dioxide which the leaf gets from the air, to manufacture sugar and starch. The plant produces other foods it needs by adding minerals from the soil.

Long ago green plants gained the ability to grow up to twice as many food-producing leaves as are needed for their own survival. Otherwise, plant eaters could never have developed.

Sphinx moth on bergamot

FOOD CHAINS

When an animal eats a plant or eats another animal, it becomes part of a food chain. In our backyard, as well as everywhere else, all food chains begin with plant-eaters (herbivores) and usually end with a meat-eater (carnivore). Food chains can be short or as long as five or six links. If you eat an apple, that is a two-link food chain. If you eat meat from a sheep or cow that has eaten plants, that is a three-link food chain. You are at the top of those food chains.

Here in the backyard, one food chain might begin with a moth sipping nectar from a flower— just like that sphinx moth on the wild bergamot plant. The moth is caught by a sparrow and fed to its young in the nest in our hedge. The young bird might be taken from its nest and eaten by a raccoon. The raccoon is at the top of this food chain. There are no predators in the backyard to eat the raccoon.

Raccoon in backyard

Sparrow at nest in hedge

Another food chain might start with a fly feeding on decaying vegetation in the backyard. The fly is caught and eaten by a spider. The spider is eaten by a toad, which is eaten by a fox.

First links in any food chain are usually the smallest but most abundant plants and animals. Microscopic green algae and other plant plankton float in the ponds, lakes, and seas. They are eaten in great quantities by water insects and small crustaceans, which are eaten by small fishes, which are, in turn, eaten by larger fishes that may end up on your dinner table.

Spider eating fly

Toad

Each time an animal eats a plant or one animal eats another, a tiny bit of the sun's energy is passed along the food chain. Each animal uses some of that energy and passes along what is left. Amazingly, the used energy is not destroyed, only changed into other forms or passed into the atmosphere. Energy and matter can't be destroyed in living things.

Fox

BALANCING POPULATIONS

Animal populations are kept in balance by the amount of food available and by predators in the food chain. Take mice, for instance. You can't really catch sight of them scurrying through the tall grass in the backyard, eating seeds. They move quickly to avoid enemies. During a summer of heavy rainfall and lush vegetation, the mouse population increases, providing more food for hawks and owls and other mouse-eaters. When

Daughter Melody feeds an injured hawk.

Barred owl

less food is available, mice tend to raise fewer young. This affects the numbers of hawks and owls also. If the insect and rodent populations decrease, owls and hawks raise fewer young or find better territory or else starve. A balance of numbers is maintained.

Some farmers shoot hawks and owls, believing that they kill a few chickens. But without these predators, rabbits and mice overpopulate and spread into cultivated fields to eat corn, wheat, oats, rye, barley, rice, and sugar cane—the grasses which are first links in human food chains. This is what happens when we upset a balanced community.

Young barn swallows in nest

FEATHERED HELPERS

Birds are a great help in keeping the numbers of insects in balance.

The friendly chickadees are greeting us from the lilac bushes, with their cheerful call…dee-dee-dee…between dashes to the feeder for sunflower seeds, or excursions into the brush for caterpillars and other insects and spiders.

A couple of barn swallows are catching winged insects to feed their babies in a mud-and-straw nest on a high beam in our garden tool shed.

A pair of cardinals is swooping down on grasshoppers. I can't help hoping that no snake or owl raids their nest in the hedge, but that's a possibility.

The tiny house wren parents are tireless hunters, making continuous trips from dawn until dark to satisfy the high-pitched hunger cries of their babies in the nest box near our kitchen win-

Wren at nest box

dow. A young bird may eat its weight in insects every day!

In the spring, we watch the birds compete for inchworms, hopping from twig to twig, picking the leaves clean.

We saw the female Baltimore oriole peel dried fibers off last year's tall dogbane plant with her beak and fly high up in the oak tree to weave them into her nest. She and the male who courted and won her fed their nestlings with soft parts of insects, and themselves ate caterpillars, beetles, wasps, grasshoppers, and ants.

Young blue jays with innocent faces and fresh white and blue feathers follow their parents around, fluttering their wings to be fed, although they've grown as large as the adults.

Birds are a joy to watch as they go about their business, protecting the plants in our backyards and gardens from an oversupply of leaf-eating insects.

KEEPING INSECTS IN BALANCE

Birds thrive on insects and so do moles and shrews, but for millions of years insect populations have kept in balance mostly by feeding on each other. To us, some of them may resemble aliens from outer space, but most of the earth's inhabitants are insects. This is true in our backyard too. Insect predators attack many insects for different meals. Let's look for some among the wildflowers —the colorful phlox, bee balm, and asters.

Lacewing larva   *Adult lacewing*

Lacewings

Lacewings are tiny insects. In their juvenile stage as larvas, they have a lizardlike shape and you would never guess that they will grow up to be delicate golden-eyed lacewings with pale gauzy wings.

Lacewings are eaten by birds, and sometimes they get caught in spider webs. But I would rather see them survive in our garden, as they are very beneficial. Lacewing larvas are called aphid-lions because of their big appetites for small, plant-sucking aphids and leafhoppers and for moth eggs.

Lacewing eggs hatching

Female lacewings lay their eggs in a special way, first depositing a drop of fluid on a leaf or stem, then raising their abdomen to pull the drop into a silky thread. If they didn't lay their eggs at the tips of these thin stalks, their firstborn might eat its own sisters and brothers as they're hatching.

A lacewing larva that has eaten plant-sucking leafhoppers might survive to become a winged adult and then get caught in a spider web and eaten. That would be a short food chain. It could get longer if that spider is eaten by a toad and the toad is eaten by an opossum.

23

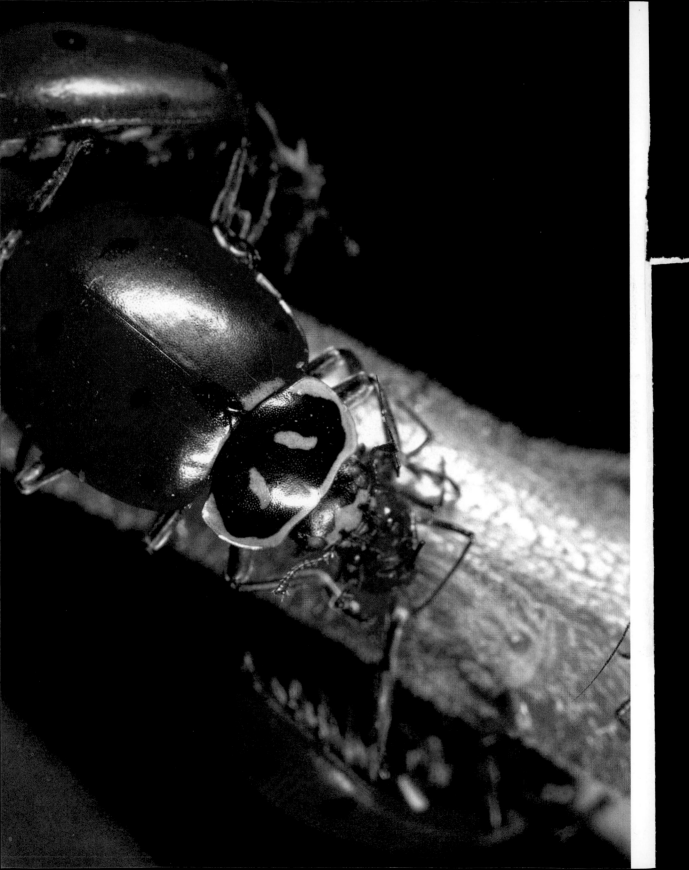

Ladybird Beetles

"Ladybug, ladybug, fly away home. Your house is on fire, your children do roam." As a child, I repeated that old chant when I saw a ladybird beetle, commonly known as a ladybug. I had no idea that both adult and juvenile ladybugs help keep insect populations in balance in the garden by devouring tiny, plant-sucking aphids, mites, and scale insects.

Orange or yellow ladybugs decorated with black polka dots are easy to recognize as they ﹍unt through foliage for prey. Various species have ﹍rent numbers of spots. They are the adults. In ﹍venile stage, ladybug larvas look something ﹍ing larvas and they're just as hungry for

﹍ugs may be attacked by a micro-
﹍t lays its eggs in the larvas.
﹍gs are not attacked, if they
﹍sucking prey, they die.
﹍lance with their food

﹍e
﹍on-
eyes

ambush position

﹍bug saved the Cal-
﹍en they were threat-

ened by the cottony-cushion scale insect that had hitched a ride from Australia. Most insects that overpopulate and make "pests" of themselves have come from somewhere else without the natural enemies which kept them in balance in their homeland. Or else their enemies were wiped out by pesticides.

Praying Mantises

Praying mantises appear fierce, but they are patient hunters waiting for their insect prey to roam within reach of their long "arms."

The barberry hedge is dotted with green berries that will turn red when the weather gets cooler. Let's examine the branches. It's easy to overlook this large, elegant, slow-moving Chinese mantis, although he grows three or four inches long.

In summer, the mantis is as green as t leaves which help him hide as he waits mot less—not in prayer, but in ambush. His big

Praying mantis in

26

detect another insect's slightest movement. Then his "arms" strike out. Their double rows of sharp spines grasp and fold over his prey like a jackknife.

Last spring, when he emerged with hundreds of his sisters and brothers from an overwintering egg case, he was tiny and pale, and lucky to avoid being eaten by ants or a bird before he himself had a chance to start catching aphids and young inchworms. As he grew, he caught crickets and larger insects. Compared with more aggressive predators, praying mantises don't eat enough insects to affect the balance very much, but their young are food for others.

Mantises mate in autumn. The female's tendency toward cannibalism at this time may seem ghastly, but consider her situation. Her abdomen is heavy with hundreds of eggs and food is scarce. The male would soon die anyway and he is very close at hand, so sometimes she devours him to provide the energy she will need to construct her egg case. During the winter, if a hungry squirrel or a chickadee comes across the egg case hidden in the hedge, it will break it open and eat the eggs.

Female mantis devouring male

Wasps

Wasps are almost as valuable as birds in helping maintain a balanced insect population. Over the course of a summer, social wasps—which live in colonies—capture huge numbers of insects. Equipped with both sucking and chewing mouth parts, they chew the insects before feeding them to the larvas in their combs. Solitary wasps stock their nests with insects and spiders as food for their larvas.

Wasps, in turn, may be eaten by birds or attacked by parasites, so their numbers are kept in balance.

Let's walk down the pleasant path to our tool shed. The path is bordered with clover, daisies, and jewelweed. Dandelions are scattered here and there. Beneath the overhang of the shed roof, you can see the uncovered paper comb of the social wasp known as Polistes. The Polistes queen began the comb by herself, laid an egg in each cell and fed insects to her first brood of larvas.

Path to the tool shed

Polistes wasp on comb

When those daughters emerged as adults, they helped enlarge the comb and feed insects to later broods.

Here's a yellow jacket, also a social wasp. She eats soft-bodied insects and overripe fruit. If you follow her, you'll discover a paper globe nest hanging under a roof. Or it may be hidden underground in an old mouse nest, and in that case you want to be careful not to step on it and rouse the colonists, as they're quick to sting if threatened.

Yellow jacket

A mud dauber wasp is visiting the wildflowers to sip their nectar, but her larvas eat spiders. If you come into the tool shed, you'll see why this solitary wasp is called a mud dauber. Up there on the wall, what seems like an organ pipe is the nest she built out of mud. In each cell, she places paralyzed spiders before she lays an egg and seals the cell. That way her larvas will have fresh "meat" when she is no longer around to feed them.

Mud dauber on nest

Cecropia caterpillar

Stink Bugs

Some stink bugs feed on plants and others feed on caterpillars such as the larvas of Cecropia giant silkworm moths. These caterpillars are also eaten by mice and by insect parasites and predators, so although they feed on cherry, maple, willow, and other trees, their numbers are kept in balance.

We found a stink bug attacking a Cecropia caterpillar in the wild cherry tree at the edge of our

Albuquerque Academy
MIDDLE SCHOOL LIBRARY
6400 Wyoming Blvd. N.E.
Albuquerque, NM 87109

woods. We didn't need a magnifying glass to see the large green caterpillar with red knobs, which was known to the native American Indians. The caterpillar had been nibbling a wild cherry leaf when it was attacked by the smaller, shield-shaped stink bug with a swordlike sucking tube which the bug extended to pierce the skin of its larger prey. Through the hollow tube, the bug sucked the caterpillar's vital fluids. The caterpillar twisted to escape, but in vain. It never became a moth.

The bug that attacked the caterpillar that nibbled the wild cherry leaf may, in turn, be eaten by a bird.

Stink bug attacking caterpillar

Dragonflies

Dragonflies are a great help in reducing mosquito populations. And what a beautiful sight—a dragonfly resting for a few moments on a stem, with wings outspread, its long, slender body sparkling in the sun like a gold and black jewel! Soon it takes off, zigzagging and darting through the air, capturing mosquitos and midges in a cage formed by its legs as it flies. Some dragonflies are metallic blue, green or red. We called them darning needles when I was a child, and we were afraid of them, although we had no reason to be, as they never do us any harm.

Two hundred fifty million years ago, there lived dragonflies with a wingspread of twenty-seven inches! Today's descendants, although much smaller, are among the more visible insects around ponds, lakes, and swamps.

Let's walk to the pond nearby to see where dragonflies and the more delicate damselflies lay their eggs on water plants. The nymphs grow up underwater where some of the larger species spend several years feeding on mosquito larvas and other small creatures which they catch by unfolding a long lower lip.

In the pond, crayfish (relatives of crabs and shrimps) mainly eat plants and are themselves eaten by fishes and dragonfly nymphs, which are, in turn, food for many larger fishes. Dragonflies are an important part of underwater food chains as both predators and prey.

A dragonfly nymph leaves the water when ready to shed its skin for the last time and emerge as a winged adult. Some die after only a few weeks. Others live throughout the summer, eating many of the mosquitos and tiny flies that would otherwise annoy us.

Spiders

Spiders are not insects, they are arachnids, with four pairs of legs. But they are hunters and trappers of insects. Their digestive juices liquify their prey before it's sucked into their mouths.

Who is this little fellow peering out of his hiding place in a curled leaf? Has this jumping spider ventured out to see who we are? His eight eyes can recognize prey four to eight inches away. When he recognizes an insect, he jumps on it and holds it down with his forelegs while his fangs inject a paralyzing fluid.

Spiders themselves are eaten by other spiders, solitary wasps, parasites, toads, frogs, birds, and shrews. Ants eat spider eggs. So spiders have many enemies to keep their numbers in balance.

Parasites

A parasite lives part of its life in or on the body of a single host. Many thousands of species of insect parasites lay their eggs inside other insects.

Come over to the Queen Anne's lace. The flowers seem like yards of white lace spun by other-worldly hands. It's a pleasure to examine their delicate florets. But here's a black swallowtail caterpillar in very bad shape! The reason is obvious. A parasitic braconid wasp has just climbed out of a cocoon on its back. This is just one of the many species of braconids. When this parasite was in its larval stage, it fed on the caterpillar's insides. Now the caterpillar is dying.

A great many other kinds of parasitic wasps attack a wide variety of insects, and some attack other parasites. We seldom notice these smallest allies that help keep insect populations in balance.

Braconid wasp and cocoon on caterpillar

PLANT AND INSECT PARTNERS

Insects are food for many kinds of creatures. We depend on insects to provide us with products such as honey and silk. Yet of all the services insects perform, the most necessary is helping plants to reproduce. Without insect pollinators, there would be far fewer plants and many of our fruits and vegetables would no longer grow. Animals would have much less to eat, and life on earth would decrease.

The fragrances, colors, and sweet nectar offered by flowers are all ways that plants attract butterflies, moths, bees, wasps, beetles, and other insects to transfer pollen grains from the stamens of one plant to the stigma of another so that the flowers can bear seeds.

We planted dahlias around the bird bath because butterflies are attracted to them. See—a tiger swallowtail has landed on one. Come closer and watch it sip nectar through its long sucking tube.

Have you ever sniffed the sweetness of a dandelion? Dandelions supply nectar to bees, yet

Tiger swallowtail on dahlia

many people destroy them with weed-killers that also harm birds, pets, and people, and continue doing harm as the poisons seep down to the water table underground and end up contaminating drinking water.

Bee collecting pollen

Here's a bee collecting pollen in the hairy "baskets" on her legs. She flies to the next flower, where some of the pollen clinging to her furry body rubs off on the flower's sticky stigma and travels down to the ovules. Pollinating insects and flowering plants could not have developed as they did without each other's help.

44

MAMMALS

A family of deer often comes out of the small woods bordering our backyard and browses among the plants. When we go outside, they stop and stare at us with wide eyes, then turn and leap gracefully away, wiggling their white tails.

In winter, they walk through the snow up to the house itself to nibble hedges and shrubs. Deer can double their numbers in a single year. Long ago, their populations were kept in check mainly by cougars (mountain lions) that leaped on them

from low tree limbs. And by packs of wolves, and by native American Indians who hunted them for food, buckskins, and doeskins. Today, without predators except man in many places, deer sometimes eat every leaf and bud in their range, and some starve in winter.

The lively little chipmunks have found an easy way to make a living. Besides collecting wild plant seeds, one is sitting near the bird feeder, stuffing so many fallen sunflower seeds into his mouth that the pouches in his cheeks puff up like small balloons. He races to his underground nest to store them away and is soon back for more, running quickly to avoid hawks and other predators.

A red fox sometimes walks stealthily into our backyard at sunset, hunting mice and birds. The chipmunks dart into their burrows where they're safe from the fox, but not from weasels.

Snowy tree cricket

As we wait for more furry visitors, the evening air is filled with scraping sounds of katydids calling their own names, and the high jingle bell chorus of snowy tree crickets. They feed on the foliage in which they hide, daring to advertise for mates at night when the birds that prey on them are asleep.

A family of raccoons and an opossum make trails through the backyard, stopping to munch berries. This is part of their regular rounds as they seek out mice, lizards, grasshoppers, crickets, and grub in the mud for frogs.

In case they're still hungry, the raccoons are bold enough to look in our kitchen window or tap on the door and invite themselves in for a snack. The opossum, who eats almost anything, gets in on the act. After all, humans have taken over much of their territory.

RESTORING A BALANCE

We humans are the only species that inter-feres in a drastic way with natural balances. We breed huge numbers of other animals, plant single crops where many kinds of plants grew before, and destroy any creatures that compete with us for territory and food—often poisoning our own surroundings in the process. The human popula-tion increases unchecked, and the air, water, and soil are so polluted by human activities that unless we learn to limit ourselves and live in harmony with our natural environment, we are in danger of destroying our planet's life-support system.

When we interfere with natural balances in our own neighborhoods—cutting down meadows, manicuring large lawns, and spraying poisons—delicate insect parasites and predators disappear. Some people help restore a balance in their back-yards and gardens by buying ladybugs and many other beneficial laboratory-raised insect predators and parasites from garden catalogs.

Japanese beetles are an example of insects that arrived on imported foods without their natu-

Japanese beetles

ral enemies. Around our raspberry bushes we hung a bag containing a lure that mimics the female Japanese beetle's scent. Male Japanese beetles attracted to it are trapped in the bag before they get a chance to mate with real females or

feed on the raspberry plants. In this way, the "pest" insect's own biology is turned against itself, and its numbers reduced.

NATURAL WASTE RECYCLING

In nature, all wastes are biodegradable. That means they are broken down into their basic elements and recycled—used over and over again.

With the help of scavengers that feed on the remains of others, and decomposers too small to see, recycling helps keep the numbers of plants and animals in balance.

For instance, as an increased number of plants depletes the soil in any part of the backyard, fewer plants are able to grow there, and there's less food for animals. When those fewer plants die, their elements are returned to the soil by earthworms, springtails, bacteria, fungi, algae, and other tiny creatures that help break down dead plants, restoring fertility. Now more plants can grow again to capture more energy from the sun and continue the natural cycle.

When the fox or raccoon or owl at the top of a food chain dies, parts of the body might be eaten by scavengers such as crows, rats, and ants. Any leftovers are broken down by bacteria and fungi and returned to the soil.

Would you like to see what's under the flat stepping-stones? We'll lift one, and uncover a colony of busy ants. When ants come across dead insects, they drag them home to feed their grubs. In this way ants recycle the stored energy and substances left in dead insects, to nourish new life.

Let's turn over a decaying log and see what's inside. It could be a colony of carpenter ants, but

Ants caring for larvas

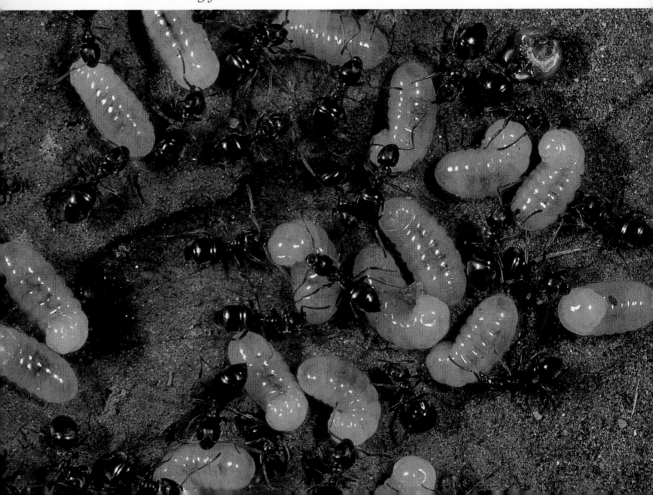

no—these tunnels were carved by termites. When termites eat dead wood, they help recycle its elements to create new soil so that new plants can grow.

In the physical world, everything is borrowed and shared and reused. The tiny building blocks that form different types of matter are called *atoms*. Plants and animals keep reusing them in different combinations that make up the compounds that form living things.

Your own body is composed of recycled materials. It is made up of carbon, hydrogen, oxygen, nitrogen, and mineral atoms. When you eat, groups of food atoms are decomposed (digested) by your body and recomposed into parts of you. Those atoms were used by other animals and plants many thousands of times before they became part of you. It's an amazing thought, but some atoms in your body might once have been part of a bird or a flower or even a dinosaur! Of course, you are a brand-new and very special individual, even though the atoms that make up your body are quite ancient.

As the poet, Alexander Pope, wrote: "All are but parts of one stupendous whole, whose body nature is, and God the soul."

We hope you have enjoyed our backyard, and seeing how plants and animals are dependent on one another. It's all part of nature's great balancing act. When you and your friends go exploring around your yards or in the park, we hope you'll keep on discovering interrelationships in the world we all share.

Glossary

Algae—Simple single-celled or many-celled plants containing chlorophyll.

Amphibians—Cold-blooded animals, such as frogs. The young live in water; adults have lungs to breathe air and live on land.

Arachnids—Arthropods with four pairs of legs and no antennae, mainly spiders.

Arthropods—Joint-legged animals, including insects, spiders, crabs and lobsters.

Chlorophyll—The green color in plants.

Crustaceans—Joint-legged animals with crustlike shells, such as lobsters.

Decomposer—That which breaks down complex materials into their basic elements.

Deplete—Reduce or use up.

Food chain—The transfer of food energy, as when one animal eats a plant or another animal and is itself eaten by still another animal. Food chains may have just a few links or many.

Kaleidoscope—An instrument through which changing patterns are seen.

Larva—The early stage of many insects, before they change form and develop into adults.

Mammals—Warm-blooded animals (including humans) that nurse their young from milk glands.

Parasite—A plant or animal that lives in or on another and feeds off it.

Pesticide—A chemical poison used to kill animals.

Pistil—The organ of a flower containing the female reproductive parts.

Plankton—Floating animal and plant life in water, usually very tiny.

Pollination—The transfer of pollen from one flower to another, resulting in the production of seeds.

Predator—One that captures and feeds on other animals.

Prey—Any animal captured for food.

Reproduction—The process by which any plant or animal makes another like itself.

Scavenger—One that feeds on dead animals which it has not itself killed.

Stamen—The pollen-bearing male reproductive part of a flowering plant.

Stigma—The top of the pistil of a flower.

Species—A group of individuals (plant or animal) of the same kind and designated by the same name.

Index

E. Jaediker Norsgaard is an artist and writer of film narrations. Her articles have appeared in *Smithsonian* and *Natural History* magazines, illustrated with her husband's photographs, and in *Ranger Rick*'s nature magazine. Her science notes accompany their fifty nature subjects distributed to schools as film cassettes.

Campbell Norsgaard, internationally known cinematographer, was featured with his nature films in the *National Geographic* TV Special "The Hidden World," and "The Backyard Jungle," and many other television shows. His documentaries include Sir Edmund Hillary and wildlife in Alaska. His film footage appears in two *Encyclopaedia Britannica* films.

Before settling in the United States, Norsgaard filmed the wartime activities of the Royal Norwegian Air Force. He and his wife live in Connecticut. *How to Raise Butterflies* was their most recent book for children.

574.5   Norsgaard, E. Jaediker
NOR   (Ernestine Jaediker)

          Nature's great
           balancing act.

                                              11468

$14.95

DATE		